RACHILDE

THE BLOOD-GUZZLER

AND OTHER STORIES

TRANSLATED BY
SUE BOSWELL

ISBN: 978-1-64525-143-9

All the stories in the present volume were taken from *Contes et Nouvelles* (1900), with the exception of "Primordial Nakedness", which first appeared in the review *Jazz*, on April 15, 1931.

THE BLOOD-GUZZLER
AND OTHER STORIES

"RACHILDE" was the pen name of Marguerite Vallette-Eymery (1860–1953), one of the most important writers of the Decadent Movement. Her works include the novels *Monsieur Vénus* (1884), and *The Princess of Darkness* (1895), the latter book being written under the pseudonym Jean de Chilra. She also wrote a 1928 monograph on gender identity, *Pourquoi je ne suis pas féministe* ("Why I am not a Feminist").

SUE BOSWELL studied French Language and Literature at UCL and for a time taught French at Goldsmiths University of London. Later she became a translator for the Wiener Holocaust Library, and translated Arnaud Rykner's novel *The Last Train* (Snuggly Books, 2020). Her other translations include *Are You All Crazy?* by René Crevel, Marcel Schwob's *The Assassins and other Stories*, Ilarie Voronca's *The Confession of a False Soul* and *The Key to Reality* and, with her husband, Colin Boswell, Gustave Kahn's *The Mad King*, also for Snuggly Books.

CONTENTS

THE BLOOD-GUZZLER

AND OTHER STORIES

THE BLOOD-GUZZLER

For Jean Lorrain[1]

I

ALL alone, all red, as if with drink, this full face of an eternal being frightened by a mystery which is perhaps nothing but the eternal despair of her own nothingness, the Moon travels over an immense sky, whose expanse seems to be doubled by the immense stretch of the heathland.

And deserted, and brown, but now with the pink of the day, as if struck by a mortal terror

---

1 Jean Lorrain (1855-1906), born Paul Duval, was a French poet and novelist of the Symbolist school.

resulting from its own silence, the heathland's unkempt tresses roll out, parted along the middle by the pale streak of a path, leading up to the sky, right down there, right up there, as far as the eye can see.

It's a lovely night, peacefully extraordinary, where there is nothing which is not calm and disconcerting.

Near and far: no-one. No large hat, no house's roof. No-one . . . except that the Moon has the look of someone!

Controlling, imperious, with a circular opening like a golden well, inhaling all the scents and all the breaths, she advances slightly sideways, swaying with a great tranquil inebriation, she sniffs the things and beings whose multiple lives, as they are extinguished, make this vertiginous deadly silence.

Amid the heather some birds, woken by her fiery light, remain motionless, their wings pulsating, their eyes fixed, contemplating her dazedly.

On the path, the small sand-snakes, making their way back to their nests, stop, lift their heads, beat the ground with their delicate tails, and watch, fascinated in their turn, the new flaring up of this hydra's jaw.

Myriads of funereal insects silently leave their holes, and some, to see it better, have put on emerald spectacles.

An hour passes, sombrely, with nothing any longer moving, but up high, slowly, nonchalantly, the face of her who died of fright is moving forward with her silent vampire's flight, seeking . . .

. . . She is seeking, for it is as if she is leaning over the heathland; she leans, very drunk, wishing to drink more; she inhales, she breathes in, she draws towards the golden well of her open mouth all that that is of blood or of spirit.

And now, down there, a small black shape is arriving by the pale path. At first it's an insect, an upright ant, a snake wriggling on its tail; then a bird, walking, dragging its wings; finally, it's a woman. She is very young, with a pale round face framed by a close-fitting round velvet bonnet, like those of the innocent girls of the poorhouses, with blonde locks escaping from the bonnet like slippery beams of light; she's wearing a full pleated skirt around her waist; her clogs are round-toed, and her hands, small satellite stars, are resting on her wide apron: she's a beautiful Breton girl with pale eyes opened wide so as not to see anything.

And she walks without knowing where to go, tottering slightly, her legs heavy, weary with an infinite torpor. She looks at the Moon, and the Moon must have seen her; her transparent face of one who has died of consumption has become darker, redder with dishonest blood, and it's as if a dismal thought is plunging the golden monster's distant parts into darkness.

The little peasant girl sits down on the heather, she can't go on, her breasts are tormented by soft pains like the rasping caresses of tickling grass. So is there no remedy for her suffering? The old grandmother who said to her: "Walk!"—does she know exactly why she should walk? You would sleep so well upon the heathland at this time, when the cricket no longer dares sing! You would sleep so well . . . and she stretches out, so tired that her eyes are closing despite her efforts to keep them open, because of the wicked angels . . .

She's fifteen years old and has been dreaming for the past three nights that she's eating earth. She's filled with a strange sickness whose name nobody can tell her. The old grandmother, a simpleton who waves her arms vaguely, all the family she has left, declares that it's caused by the moon, and, gesticulating with her arm towards the Ocean, beyond the deserted heathlands, she repeats:

"Yes, *she's* the one who makes the sea recede, *she's* the one who makes the women come . . ."

As the old woman is deaf, she doesn't hear the girl's incredulous laugh; she keeps her arm stiffly raised, her gaze fixed, standing before the window where the *Enemy* shines, the Blonde severed Head eternally seeking all the blood shed from her former body.

"Walk! Walk!" cries the old woman. "Go on then! It's the Moon causing it all!"

She shakes her fist, perhaps at the Moon, perhaps at the girl, and the girl, afraid, leaves, no longer bothering to laugh, for the hour of the hobgoblins has sounded for the heathland.

. . . The child cannot fight the sleep which is overcoming her, she falls asleep. This time she dreams that the Moon is kissing her, that the Moon has a mouth of honey.

"It's *she* who makes the sea recede, do you hear, Marivonnec!"[1]

When the poor girl awakens it's completely dark; and she weeps, all alone in her virginal surprise, she weeps because the Moon no longer lights up her path, and especially because no-one loves her.

Miserably she turns away, a small shadow leaving dark shadows on the pale pathway; she turns, weeping, but up high, hidden beneath the sky's gloom, the Moon must be smirking, the Moon, the fire flower, who lives off the blood of women! . . .

II

"Hi! Marivonnec? . . ."

"Hi! Jeanivon? . . ."

And they wave their arms, not knowing what else to do. He's almost eighteen years old.

---

1 A Breton version of the French name Maryvonne. Jeanivon also appears to be a regional variation of the name Jean.

Now that she feels like a woman, and pretty, she wears her fifteen years and her full pleated skirt around her waist more proudly. He's wearing a hat with a wide brim which he has inherited and that makes his face look like that of a bright-eyed chubby baby.

They walk, following the heathland's straight path, listening to the cricket. The Moon rises alone. She watches them from the horizon, crouching down at the level of the heather, the twigs giving her a moustache, and she watches them as a large cat's eye would watch two mice.

"Oh, the Moon! . . ." says Jeanivon.

"Yes, the Moon! . . ." says Marivonnec.

She remains thoughtful. There is a secret between her and the Moon, but that's no concern of Jeanivon's.

The wave their arms.

An hour passes by. The Moon rises, rises, like an amber globe in which a heart burns, like an alabaster urn full of warm ashes. She is less enormous and more pale. She's flirtatious: with a stole of white vapours beneath which her colour softens until it takes on shades of hortensia. She rises and suddenly becomes resplendent, cleared of her vapours, beautiful as the face of the bride whose veil falls away.

"Yes, the Moon! . . ." says Jeanivon, thoughtful in his turn.

"Oh, the Moon! . . ." says Marivonnec joyfully, abruptly.

They stay there, in the middle of the path, holding hands, amid a silence which delights them and the cricket himself respects their rapture.

"You have cheeks like roses!" Jeanivon hazards tenderly.

"You have cheeks like the sun," replies Marivonnec, "but you have no beard, you look like our priest!"

And she can't help laughing, she chortles, she wriggles, she rolls over and she drags Jeanivon over the heather. Jeanivon is laughing too, although it's no fun for him to be compared to a priest.

The Moon, on high, seems to be grimacing with the same forced laughter, beyond two shadows which bloom upon her surface like two waterlily flowers upon the surface of a yellow lake.

When they've finished laughing they kiss, silently, mouth on mouth, embrace each other tightly, Breton-style, without taking a breath, like doves, beak on beak, one following the other's movements, their necks rippling, swollen with pleasure. Thus do the most chaste of fiancés kiss; unfortunately, this evening the Moon has laughed . . . and Jeanivon, with a supple movement of his loins, has Marivonnec on her back. Ah! So she says he doesn't look like a man, shall he show her?

Marivonnec, the innocent one, cries out with pain whilst the Moon continues to smirk . . . the Moon, the fire flower who lives off the blood of women!

III

Clouds are galloping past in the squally weather, and behind these devil's black stallions can be seen, for a moment, the shining of the crescent Moon which digs its heels into their rumps like a golden spur. They are so low, these clouds, that they seem to hang over the heather, still brown and dark like pools of dried blood. The wind sounds like the flapping of shrouds. All the dead must be struggling, on this night, and weeping long torrents of tears over their past crimes.

Marivonnec has come out, nevertheless, because the grandmother has said to her, waving her fist at the sky:

"Go on, walk, walk, you must walk because of your sickness!"

Pushed outside by the idiotic old woman Marivonnec has come out, hiding her face under her hair which she no longer wishes to comb.

So it's still good for all ills, to walk? She realises she is being turned out, but she wants to believe too that it's a remedy, the eternal remedy; walking straight ahead! And she goes. The clouds go more quickly than she does. They bump into each other, they climb onto each other, rear up, then rush off in all directions. All that remains are some grey flakes, some shreds of wool, some feathers, some fluttering down and in the centre of the cleared battlefield the

Moon, very slender, who seems to stop, to pick herself up like the end of a bright scythe above the head of the reaper.

Marivonnec sobs. She is exhausted. It's as if someone is leading her by her belly which is so large that it's always ahead of her on the path. For three days she's been suffering without daring to cry out. Ah! The heather is not soft in winter; yet she would very much like to sleep.

Marivonnec eventually finds a bed. It's a dip in the marsh in the middle of the heathland, the rain has hollowed it out, the mud softens it and the witch will bless it . . . so what! Marivonnec stretches out, rolls over, she laughs, laughs enough to break her teeth, she howls, calls upon the evil angels. Ah! . . . All the evil angels to set her free! And *one* comes and with his pointed finger tears open her belly. Then she is furious, she is drunk with anger, she seizes him by the throat, he's quite tiny; but the worst demons are all small, and she strangles him without the slightest idea, poor girl, that she's strangling her own child.

She comes out of the ditch, covered in filth, covered in mud, bent in two, suddenly old, and she imitates the grandmother, the idiot woman; she shakes her fist at the Moon.

The latter, victorious over the black squadrons of the clouds of death, sparkles, stretches like a white flame, pure, pure like the light of a white candle. The Moon shines; the Moon, the fire flower which lives off the blood of women! . . .

THE FROG-KILLER

For Eugène Demolder[1]

SMALL, light, lying like a water insect on his pale sheet, in the night, as if on a pool of clear pond water, the boy is listening. A finger has woken him, it seems to him, a moist finger rubbing his forehead.

It is not God's finger, because God is too old now to bother with children. Silence has replaced him. God is frail now, no longer able to gallop on the wind, and He has put the wind in the stable where sometimes it growls behind the door.

---

1 Eugène Demolder (1862-1919) was a Belgian novelist, short story writer and art critic who also trained in law.

The great silence, with its cold forefinger, has woken this boy who is listening, surprised, finding really dark what he can't hear.

Crouching on all fours, his small thin limbs stiff like corn stalks, the thighs long, the knees firm, the feet narrow and looking ready to hop about, to become even narrower, he is gazing fixedly with his head lowered shiftily, his hair hanging like heavy rain across his temples with lines darker than the night, and beneath the hair his staring eyes shine like two lamps veiled in crepe, for this small undressed boy nevertheless has a mournful look.

He leads the life of an animal, coming, going, eating, sleeping, saying nothing. He has a corner of the bedroom, a dirty corner, to the right of the hearth. There he is at home like a cricket. In winter he is warm close to the embers. In summer he gets air through a hole in the roof. His bed is a willow frame solidly linked to old chair legs. Onto it had been thrown a straw mattress and a sheet . . . the same one for the past year. Very craftily, the boy shakes this sheet every morning when his mother is boiling their soup, because he's noticed that fleas don't like flames and all the vermin get burnt or drowned in the cooking pot.

But, on this June night, it is not the fleas which have woken him. He has sensed someone walking about in the distance, without making any noise. Perhaps the wind has escaped from God's stable? Or else there's a weasel? Or else a rat, one of those large field rats, brown, thick, with a smooth snake-like tail? No, no-one . . .

And the boy moves forward a little on hands and knees, lowers his head further, raises his behind. If necessary he could be upright in the middle of the bedroom in a single bound by straightening his knees. He knows that at night people don't go for walks as they do in the daytime. In the daytime animals are what they want to be, but at night they do what they can, and when birds have closed their eyes other unknown animals take their wings and leave in extraordinary leaps, skimming over the ground. He knows that, and other things too, this small ten-year-old who is left to hang around outside the house with nothing to do, only coming in to sleep and eating whatever he can find, things which make his lips bleed.

There is nothing to be heard; except, to-wards the gorse fence protecting the garden—cabbages, turnips, a beautiful onion plant—*the earth cried out*. The earth's way of crying out is really *terrible*. It's a dumb person who emits only grindings of teeth. If someone, a man or an animal, does something forbidden, it tries to give a warning and, more faithful than a good dog, it doesn't spoil things with useless shouting; gravel rolling, sand being trampled, the imperceptible sound of a snail shell being squashed are enough for it.

And still small bones of the dead are being crushed in all sorts of places, for the earth is full of them. And the small bones of the dead protest!

There was certainly someone coming from the direction of the vegetable garden. A thief? For the onions no doubt. Little Toniot jumped up in his usual way, the leap of an insect or a toad, naked from top to toe, his penis and ears erect. He thought of waking his father, big Toniot, who was sleeping in their second bedroom, beneath the hunting rifle hanging on the wall, big Toniot so exhausted from his last hunting expedition.

But was it worth shaking awake such a tired man, who had finished by going off to sleep alone, against the usual custom.

Little Toniot was not thinking of his mother, because for him, a man of ten years, women didn't count. He despised them. His mother beat him, and he would laugh, silently, behind her back, for women spread their fingers when hitting you, so nothing but air would slap your face; you hear the sound of the smack, but it hardly hurts; whilst men, they hit you with their fists; big Toniot would hit him like that, and he had a lot of respect for his father, who besides was the owner of a real hunting rifle.

Certainly, it was the thief who was coming, the onion thief. Little Toniot could no longer be mistaken. The small bones of the dead were protesting. The boy's light body, damp with the sweat of broken sleep, curled up at the corner of a chest of worm-eaten wood in which were stuffed the bread and bacon, those two treasures of the home. He looked like a little wet cat watching a large rat despite being numb with fear, and his carnivore's instinct gave him a sharp desire to sniff out the prey. If the prey turned out to be much bigger than him, he could discreetly call big Toniot . . . as the earth complains when it is trampled upon.

From his corner little Toniot could no longer see anything. The bedroom had no other window than the door and the hearth's opening. During the day the sun's rays came in through the door. The moon stuck to the hearth's opening on certain evenings, passing her white hands down through the soot, caressing the hanging cooking pot and making it shine like silver. This moon always woke little Toniot, who could *hear her shining*. Ah! Why did she not appear whilst his teeth were chattering with fear at the corner of the chest? The light is so good! And now she was miraculously opening the door, the door locked on the inside. Yes, it was the moon, like a natural person, a beautiful woman looking pale against the blackness of the night, a totally naked woman, a little chubby, her hips rounded and full, her throat high and hard, her face veiled with red hair.

Toniot had never been afraid of animals, nor females, but he was terrified by the moon disguised as a woman. He automatically brushed aside the black hair from his stubborn child's forehead, and with indescribable fright he saw the gesture reflected on the moon's forehead, as he would have seen it reflected in a mirror.

And it was not the moon, this great white reflection of himself: it was his mother. Little Toniot did not dare move.

"So what's this? Whatever are you doing there, little toad? So you're not asleep at this time of night?"

The female, confronting her little one, grumbled dully.

"I'm not doing anything at all," he replied, protecting his cheek with his raised elbow.

"Why are you awake, vermin? What are you up to there? And your father, wherever he is! Have you woken your father, wretch?"

"No, I woke myself up, because I heard something cracking in the garden."

"Is that the first time there's been cracking in the garden, little swine? At night, there's cracking everywhere! Do you have to grab all the passing noises by the tail, like a nosy parker?"

"I thought it came from over by the onions! It was as if a man's foot! . . ."

"A man's foot? Little bastard!"

And before little Toniot had thought to lift his elbow, the female grabbed him by the shoulders in a rage and pushed him towards his straw mattress, the corner of the pigsty from which the wretched little pig should not have emerged before time. There, blindly, without speaking, clenching her fists this time, and in the grip of anger she beat the boy, even though he had done nothing wrong.

Completely naked, the child bore the blows to his vulnerable places, without crying, in accordance with his disdainful custom, and, that night, it seemed to him the least complaint might get him killed.

The mother seemed to be drunk.

"I'll tie you up, vermin," she repeated, quietly, clenching her teeth and even more her fists. "I'll tie up your paws like a chicken for sale!"

Then he replied, equally quietly, guessing that he had to submit, obeying an order coming from higher than the blows:

"So, what? Are you angry? Why aren't you wearing your nightdress? Stop it, or you'll wake him up."

The female stopped suddenly, throwing back her hair.

Little Toniot imitated her.

They looked at each other from the depths of the darkness where the panting body of the mother gave off a sort of light. And each was ashamed of their nudity.

Crouching on his sheet, feeling his hot limbs which would be blue by the morning, the boy watched the female with anguished curiosity, protecting his small penis with his left hand, for he suspected that if she hit him again down there that would be the end of the *little toad*, which would croak and then be dead.

And why did she start hitting out like a man now? Are naked women entitled to everything? So what mystery had just come into the bedroom with a clear skin? And he shivered with fear.

"Ah, I'm more tired than if I'd laid you like an egg, you spawn!" muttered the mother, turning her back on him to go and put on her nightdress.

It was as if the moon was finally leaving them. The darkness came back and Toniot breathed again.

※

Big Toniot was scrawny, dirty. He had the sad look of a wolf who's thrown everything up, eating into itself for lack of anything better. His grey-brown canvas trousers, now green because of their long rubbing against the forest moss and the grassy slopes, slipped pathetically past his skinny hips, leaving visible between his belt and a short patched jacket a strip of fawn leather which was its owner's skin. (Little Toniot, in imitation of his father, would draw a similar strip on himself by means of a ligature, and would tighten the string until he bled in order to make a clear demarcation.) This man did not speak. He killed animals, a *mole-catcher* by trade. He set traps for foxes, ferrets, rats, fish, and especially game, and as he did not have a hunting permit he took a few precautions, such as having as an indicator moles, often weeks old and rotten, conspicuously hanging from the back of his jacket.

He had inherited his house, hidden away in a clearing of this wood, like a shipwrecked sailor on a desert island; he lived there simply, catching anything that could be eaten: the woman and the little boy could not ask for more, since the police didn't get involved. From time to time he would go off towards the next town, very far away, to sell a few baskets of rushes. Out of five baskets he would always bring back one carefully filled with horse manure, to encourage the vegetables in the garden. He would also buy bread and bacon which he placed in the middle of the manure covered with old newspaper because of the flies. He walked barefoot winter and summer, the soles of his feet having become as hard as iron. It wasn't clear whether he loved his wife. His wife had a visceral hatred for him. For one thing, he didn't talk and women have a superstitious horror of silence; and then he'd given her a son when she would have preferred a daughter, that is to say, an ally, an accomplice, a more supple being, capable of understanding all the pointless sentences that flow from exasperated mouths on rainy days. Besides, big Toniot's female complained about him with an abundant torrent of froth to the occasional women passing by on a Sunday which Providence deigned to send her. When the shepherdesses or the women gathering dead wood or lilies of the valley or peddling small wares would wander as far as her house then there would be a flood of words and lamentations driving them with arms swinging all around the house, from which the two males had been instantly evicted. Thankfully, the big and the small Toniots were able to get well away, the woods being enormous; and during this time the red-headed female, tired of the lazy life she was leading between these two evil boys ("so evil, Madame, that they click their teeth without ever saying anything") would express her unhappiness and how she could no longer decently sleep beside her man, *he stank so much of moles*.

Then, enjoying unnecessary expense, she would buy a bundle of firewood, some mushrooms gathered the day before, a bunch of lilies of the valley or two pence worth of yarn.

Big Toniot never reprimanded her for it, but little Toniot would shake his head, scornfully. Did they not have enough leisure for gathering their own firewood, their mushrooms, even their lilies of the valley themselves? As for the yarn, he, little Toniot, knew how to make it, with twigs whose toughness he had many times experienced when making snares for birds.

One Sunday it was a pedlar man instead of the door-to-door saleswoman who sold some yarn to big Toniot's wife. That day the talk was not so loud in the empty house . . . The pedlar unfolded some material. It was very interesting. You could have heard the bees making honey, and big Toniot, the following week, noticed someone was stealing his onions.

"How can you," cried the female, bristling all over, "how can you accuse a decent pedlar man who follows the police rules, who has even shown me his sales licence! He doesn't even need your onions, you piece of filth! He's a real gentleman, wears shoes every day and drinks wine on Sundays."

What she was not admitting was that she had given the onions in exchange for a few other shady courtesies.

Big Toniot looked down, sniffing from near the door. There was a smell of wine there, and he said no more, since each word would cost him a mental effort. Besides, when he was watching an animal prowling around behind a hedge he was not childish enough to make speeches at it!

But little Toniot promised himself naively that he would keep an eye on their onions.

That is why, when he had heard *cracking* not far from the garden, he had got out of bed one night, whilst the father was sleeping below his hanging gun, his father, the male relegated by a female who had become extremely delicate since she had been wanting a nightdress and could no longer bear the irritating contact of a shirt on her burning skin . . .

Alas! Little Toniot has a fever now, he doesn't sleep. It is his turn to hunt the big beast. He sniffs. He listens in the darkness. He turns and turns again softly on the dried straw for fear of making a noise. Each night he waits for something. Something or someone. He doesn't really know. The forefinger of silence digs around in his brain. He has worked out that it is once a week that one hears the earth complaining. Dull groans of a breast being knelt upon, a deep shuddering of disgust which fades to a discreet signal like the cough of a very old but polite person; and the earth's heart beats in the breast of the little watching wild creature, who finally gets up, looks straight ahead of him, his nostrils sniffing the trail.

With a snake's lithe movement little Toniot has reached the door without examining his mother's bed. He well understands that Madam Moon is out. What remains there is the canvas shirt lying on the brown blanket, the shroud of her who died bringing him into the world a second time beneath the blows of her powerful fists.

Ah! She made him a man that dreadful night, and he has well understood that he was becoming her enemy for always.

To the hunt!

And he slips outside into the soft clear blue light which bathes him, caresses him, fills him with waves of courage. The moon is hidden over by the pond where the frogs are singing. Yes, the moon is there upon the lower branches of the woods. She makes a pretty white shape, completely round, rolling along at the level of the grass; she is veiled by a thick cloud around her waist hoping to eat her head. And she rolls, she slides, and rays of light emanate from her, reflections of red hair, of a pale milky throat. Little Toniot creeps along, cautiously crushing the grass. He has passed through the garden, he's close to the ditch, in front of the wood where there is a sort of alcove, a wide blanket of greenery. He watches, he watches, and laughs silently, despite the dreadful tightening of his heart. What he sees, he will never forget, because it is so funny! He sees a large white frog, yes, that's really what it is, that wonderful flexibility of the thighs and the open arms, that supple and precise stretching of limbs so pale that they appear silvery! Now he understands why they call him *toad*, it's because he really is the son of a frog. He watches, he watches, it makes his eyes hurt, they sting! He'll watch that all his life, inside himself, in the middle of his heart, he'll be mirrored in it as if in a poisoned stream whose reflections are at once cruel and gentle.

He really has seen enough! He goes back over his tracks, the little wild animal, he retreats back into his den. Perhaps he'll go back to bed like a docile and obedient child, his face turned to the wall, but it is stronger than him, the spirit of the earth, the ancient pact agreed between man and man for protection against Her, the Enemy, pushes him past his bed as far as his father's bed.

Big Toniot awakes in his turn, sniffing the air:

"What is it boy, are you ill?"

"No, it's mother, you need to go there. Get up quickly Daddy."

He said *Daddy* like when he was a little child, not capable of doing anything bad.

And the father gets up, snorts, sniffs:

"What now? What's she up to, the bitch?"

"They're stealing our onions, I'm sure!" adds little Toniot, his voice as low as his look, full of disgust at the inexplicable crime which he explains as best he can.

"Good God!"

And the father has unhooked his gun.

"It's the yarn pedlar eh?"

"I don't know. There's a man."

"But I know. Stay here."

The boy stays. It's no longer anything to do with him. The father knows his business.

And he goes back to bed, little Toniot, blocking his ears. He can hear even so: two shots, still inside himself, in the depths of his being where forever will be displayed the sight of the great white frog, of Madam Moon spreadeagled on the ground beneath an unknown cloud. He detects a cry, two cries . . . and he unblocks his ears. His teeth are chattering. What's happening, my God? Is she going to come back furious and kill him with her fists?

She does come back in fact, dragged by the hair by big Toniot.

"Little one," says the father, his voice hoarse and sounding as if all the suffering earth sighs there, "I'm bringing back some meat for you!"

The thighs of the great white frog are striped with spurts of blood from her mouth. Her arms and legs are twitching nervously as they did a little while ago, so much do the agonies of death resemble the raptures of sensuality.

Then she grinds her teeth.

The great white frog will never sing again.

❈

He has remained all alone, fairly happy with himself. His days are spent watching animals.

The gendarmes, when they took away his father, left him the gun. His mother is buried far away. The kind women who had rushed, great buzzing insects, to bring him eggs, milk, comfort, pitying his orphan's misery, have fled because he showed them, rather brutally, his horror of chatty people. He does his small amount of housework, shakes out his sheet, steeps his soup. He has plenty of room, almost everything has been sold on the judge's orders, and when the priest comes with his blessings Toniot scampers off via the chimney after bolting his door. Ah, no way, he's the master here, no longer a child going to Sunday school!

Now that he's lucky enough not to owe anything to anyone on earth, it seems to him pointless to put up with threats from heaven. (Besides, as soon as it rains he goes to bed, that way he always saves at least one meal!)

However, the seasons are changing. He's going to have to go to the prison to get his father's togs, for his lad's trousers don't want to grow with him. First he makes two baskets with rushes, remembering the kit they used to put together for trips into town . . . and hides two rabbits in them. The rabbits and the baskets, one inside the other, are probably worth around one hundred sous. A fortune. Grub for six months.

So he leaves, taking a load of paths willy-nilly. He'll still arrive and he has plenty of time. And indeed, he arrives; it's the town's market day. He mentions big Toniot, he who killed his wife . . . Everyone still remembers what that's all about. That surprises him. There must be so many big Toniots who kill their wives, no? He learns that it's less frequent in the towns than you would think. Of course! There are far more . . . *frogs* than men, that's obvious, and you'd need too much lead.

He finds the prison and takes his inheritance: the famous grey-brown canvas trousers, greener than ever, decorated with reddish stars, and the old short, patched jacket. They explain some things to him: in all, his father was perhaps not so guilty; he had acted almost in accordance with his rights, and he would surely not have been sentenced to forced labour in perpetuity if he had been a gentleman of the town rather than a feral woodsman and unlicensed hunter. So, killing a wife, crippling a pedlar, that's less serious than not having a hunting permit? . . . This final echo of a civilised existence throws him into a new daze. Everything was getting mixed up in his poor simple boy's head. He throws his rabbits onto a dung heap, not daring to sell them. It makes him dizzy. It's as if he's thrown his father and mother there. He gives his baskets away randomly, flees from the town as if he had the whole police force at his heels, and only breathes again deep in the woods. So he really has to live without a hunting permit? So then what? He'll have to provide them more often with explanations for his personal gunshots?

He finds a way round it. Instead of killing rabbits or people, he'll go fishing, that's all. The main thing is to stay free. And thinking of what he'll fish for, he laughs silently . . .

. . . For they're still singing, the whores! As soon as night falls they're heard jabbering, croaking, deep in all the forest pools, the pools surrounding his house, the lovely pools, goblets of glaucous crystal overflowing with mosses, full of a mysterious liquid containing equal portions of autumn's poisonous fallen leaves and the purest honey of spring's flowers, irises, water lilies, arrowgrasses and periwinkles, dark periwinkles winding into pigtails to ensnare the legs of those tracking animals.

Yes, yes, they were murmuring, the whores, imploring, howling their undying pain at seeking themselves a king, and, whilst gathering in filthy circles, shining with the pleasure of their loud stupidity, they were disturbing him with their sinister vociferations. From all corners of the woods, on summer evenings, arose a concert of curses showering the orphan's forehead with seemingly endless sobbing.

Ah! Yes, he well knew what he would be fishing for! Since you have to kill to live, it's better to kill noiselessly and that the death one brings should stifle all the noise. What joy it will bring him to gather those living flowers of the murky pools, blooming in the jaws of the mad ones . . . which he'd close one by one.

Coming back from the town, little Toniot felt from now on like a big Toniot, a little more of a savage than the other one, having inherited a deserted house and an assassin's trousers. And he stood tall, finding respect for himself, as a man who has found his way. The rush baskets scarcely make anything, the mushrooms don't last, and the birds are strangely wary. The rats from the field make a poor roast, giving off when cooked a fetid smell of musk . . . Whilst a frog . . . that's like chicken! A real feast! He would see, in a happy dream, the small white thighs arrayed on a hazelwood skewer, browning in the fire and turning like obedient little puppets, vaguely ghostlike. He would eat a lot of them and would sell the rest. Finally, he would rid the countryside of these aggravating little creatures, whose songs, half prayers, half swear words, the litanies of hysterics, hideously obsessed his memory.

. . . Every day Toniot leaves his house where the winter wind has done its worse, carrying away a door and part of the roof. It's no longer his inherited house, it's his ruin. He lives there like a night bird huddling after a tempest in the hole in an old wall or a rock. He has lost all interest in light or in bread. He only comes awake with the first cries of the frogs. Then he crouches on all fours, like a savage on the war path, sniffing the wind. He creeps along, he snuffles, he breathes in the scents of the forest which the morning is tenderly moistening with its tears. If it's autumn, there's a smell of rosemary, juniper and acorns which as they dry exhale small whiffs of bitterness. If it's spring, the scent is of sage, elderberry and fully blossoming dog roses.

The animals either begin to run away or they mingle together wildly.

The only difference happening with the man is a little more sadness or a little more lethargy.

Nothing is obvious and everything would make you so sad, if you thought about it.

But Toniot has already given up thinking. He is far from the towns, far from his parents, far from himself. But the dangerous pools, mirrors reflecting all mysteries, fascinate him, bewitch him. He is the prince of the frogs which hail him with frantic passion . . . without ever having glimpsed him for longer than the time it took to die.

And he approaches them, with his fishing rod on his shoulder from where there hangs a piece of string (perhaps sold long ago to his mother by the pedlar!) and a small piece of red cloth the length of a woman's tongue. He moves along with a methodical step beneath the branches, his stare cold and fixed, his black hair in hard lines across his forehead. He has the look of a very old man with the piercing gaze of a young animal. At the pool he greets them with his silent laugh. He makes no speech to them, nor gives them any sign of his joyful arrival. They all, in their great numbers, spread out, and begin to undulate in wide clusters, making the water ripple like soft silk.

Around them the trees watch the drama, lowering their heads. Their tearful hairstyles unravel and the moon, which appears early when the sky is clear, shows as an amber diadem gradually darkening to the colour of blood. Later it will look like an arrowhead, sharpening with the dying of the day.

The racket of the frogs grows frighteningly, their yellow eyes, drops of weeping gold, light up like stars. From the midst of their witches' sabbath they cry out with human words, their piercing exclamations are like those of children having great fun or bawling themselves hoarse with puerile anger. They are small aborted babies born of forbidden love affairs, small foetuses plunged into the globe of the universe and trying to break through its glass with their small despairing hands.

And now here they are, piling into one another, poor little monsters, to look at the red tongue which the man is poking at them from the end of his wretched fishing rod. It's the fiery tongue of dreams! He has been fascinated by them, charming little sirens, and he in turn fascinates them. The rod lifts up, the string whips through the air, and a horrible cry of a bird being plucked alive is heard. The frog, overly curious, is seized by the double bait which, from a distance, appears like an anchor of salvation. It kicks its little back legs like those of a girl being raped . . .

The frog hunter gathers them up one by one, calmly.

He seems to sweep them up with the end of his fishing rod. He would take them all if it were possible to take all the frogs from a pool where each drop of sludge conceals another one about to hatch, and each drop of clear water carries an adult. But night is falling.

The moon watches, a queen who happily mocks what is happening with her subjects. Whether the frogs sing or die, that doesn't prevent her being the only frog's eye which has seen everything since the world began.

THE DEATH OF ANTINOUS[1]

<hr />

1 A favourite and probable lover of the Roman emperor
Hadrian, who ordered him to be deified upon his death
before the age of twenty.

For Henri de Régnier[1]

AT the hour when silence falls, perfumed with the dying of the roses, the hour when the air, tinted blue and coming from the distant mountains, beats its dampened wing, dampening eyelids, when the sands of warm gold bite the constricted toe with their crunching teeth, during that very hour when men no longer dare to dream for fear of opening their arms, the emperor Hadrian, he who is weakened by a cruel illness, came down towards the river, leaning on the naked shoulder of his favourite.

---

1 French symbolist poet (1864-1936).

THE EMPEROR. I have a fever! Perhaps this cool wind will calm it. Yes, I still have a fever and I don't understand it. You should explain it to me, you who are a god appointed by me, you who are the first of my slaves. You are a god and I am a king, do you hear me? We are equals. Speak!

ANTINOUS. What a fine evening, Lord.

THE EMPEROR. I want you to give me a response.

ANTINOUS. I'm listening to you Lord.

THE EMPEROR. Do you not feel your shoulder becoming rounder beneath the palm of my hand? I am your master.

ANTINOUS. The air is so soft . . .

THE EMPEROR. No. The air is heavy. You can breathe all the Nile's poisons in it. That river down there, it's also war. I'll get back on my horse, and it will have to recede. I'll have it imprisoned between two walls higher than the highest of its spates. I no longer want to see it twisting in front of this palace like a wounded enemy casting spells. But still, building walls takes time. Impatience is gnawing at me. Oh!
. . . Everything takes too long for this time of

immobility which is getting me nowhere. I have a fever, I, the master of the empire, and you can die of a fever. I shall follow the advice of my soothsayers. They claim that to purify dirty waters it's enough to whip them with silken whips steeped in the moon's water, that is to say, in the sap of celandines. Ah! . . . Really, this air is stifling me! I'm suffocating!

ANTINOUS. May the gods protect emperor Hadrian.

THE EMPEROR. You protect me then Antinous! Poor god! I've found you here as you were when I left you: a child. You are still my son and that is why I speak to you of my thoughts. I am ill, my son, I'm suffering from a strange illness more frightening than a wound. A dull sound of battle lingers deep in my ears. That stuns me and inebriates me quite differently from the aromatic wines that we used to drink on the terraces. I shall go away again. Some force is pushing me to destroy everything. But I'm happy to have seen you for a final time. You are a young tree, a tall flower . . . I am happy and I'm worried. Flowers worry because they fade. I don't know what you love and I don't know where I will go tomorrow. I am pursued by unseen archers whose soft arrows buckle against my skin, not daring to penetrate my heart. The gods want this torment. You are a god. Ah! The air is hot, the air is too hot this evening! These violent smells, these savage smells are not coming from the Nile. At the place where you go to bathe, towards nightfall, I've told them to burn incense since the dawn. It is the smells of corpses which haunt me, all the pestilence of war. I remember . . . in the tumult of arms, amongst my leaping soldiers, in the smoke of fires, my horse . . . Mind that pebble! Why walk with bare feet? You're not wearing your purple sandals? Should a god forget his sandals? You have no respect for yourself, Antinous, and you disobey me.

ANTINOUS. Only my feet are free, Lord. They lead me on despite myself.

THE EMPEROR. A strange adventure my son! My horse's legs get caught up in the entrails of a gutted elephant, pulling them, unrolling them, dragging them, and still galloping their furious gallop. At first it seemed to me that I was trampling living flesh and I wasn't surprised, I'm used to that; but when I turned round I noticed all this stinking stuff behind me like long winding reptiles and I saw blood flowing that was blue! I carried this horror with me all through the battle. I still have its frightful stink in my nostrils, it's given me the fever. Yes, the river rolls along with its dead serpents. The river is full of rotten flesh . . . That pollutes the wind's pure gusts. Everything around me is polluted! The perfume of incense is the aroma of the tomb. All the prison vents exhale filthy breaths. Feeding prisoners is useless. If you wish to live in peace, you have to suppress all the complaining. What does that presage Antinous? My horse's passage blocked, his poor legs quivering . . . He had to be put down, the beloved animal, the knots of the vile hydra were clinging to him so tightly. I think —the wind is burning me—that to live better you have to isolate yourself . . . annihilate the world, kill everything, even your horses!

ANTINOUS. You should spare your horses, Lord. The world is large.

THE EMPEROR. Don't walk so quickly . . . And the young Jewish girls taken from inside the tents, the beautiful Jewish girls which I had my soldiers offer to you? I'd given the order for their eyes to be put out . . . *afterwards*.

ANTINOUS. Your orders were faithfully executed, Lord. I heard them crying out, but without having seen them.

THE EMPEROR. You didn't want to look at them? You no longer deign to inspect my presents! So what use will my victories be? You're a child, you know nothing. Could you not amuse yourself heating up steel needles in the flames of your fire? They told me and I didn't want to believe it; it's not natural at your age. Your mouth is too melancholic. I've seen it when you're sleeping, often, as if you were no longer breathing. What do you dream about, when you dream, if not about pleasure? I want you to be full of joy. A god's sadness could be frightening. The girls were very beautiful. The most beautiful one—they found her in her father's coffer, covered by a mound of gold— shine like a piece of amber. Her hair dangling over her forehead, her teeth showing through her terrified smile and her eyes with their fixed gaze weeping at the light, she resembled a beast of the forest. Those women increase the size of their eyes by counting the stars. Their fingers are so laden with rings that they can no longer comb their hair. They hide their hair beneath bonnets of dyed hemp and once they're rich they no longer touch it. Strange slaves of love, my son. They possess the secrets of love philtres. In Rome, there are none such people since my new edicts. That's why I sent them to you. Do you know exactly what became of them?

ANTINOUS. I don't know Lord. They can't have gone very far with their eyes put out.

THE EMPEROR. Ah! . . . They'll have thrown themselves into the water . . . I'm sure of it now! They'll have gone like crawling creatures to poison my river! I can guess it from the fire drying out my breast. I've put guards all along the Nile, but there aren't any at the place where you bathe. They'll have thrown themselves into it there. They saw you and want to see you again in death. Death, it's not a barrier to love. One is never completely dead when one loves. Guards! Call my guards! I want them to look for those girls in the thickest part of the slime, do you hear me? And they can drag them into the desert.

ANTINOUS. Lord, you have forbidden your soldiers to walk along the water's edge. You're getting upset for nothing.

THE EMPEROR. Indeed, I remember . . . I forbade the guards . . . it's that it's not possible to put their eyes out. They are good servants. They need a pretext. I used to know a blind slinger who aimed well by aiming haphazardly . . . My head is bursting, Antinous. Did I drink marjoram in my wine? The fever . . . the fever!

ANTINOUS. Lord, calm down. The wind is dropping. The sand is damp. Come here! I'll show you some wonderful flowers. They're floating near the riverbank, with no stems and no leaves, like empty eggs. You'll see my usual ibises and the large lotus flowers. I'll sing for you through the reeds.

THE EMPEROR. I don't want to see anything! I don't want to hear anything! You have betrayed me, or you will betray me! Go away! . . . My fever is easy to explain and there's no need for the predictions of my astrologers. What did you do with the Jewish girls, tell me? Especially that one with flesh the colour of amber?

ANTINOUS. I swear to you, Lord, I didn't look at them.

THE EMPEROR. You didn't look at them, but you think about them, you rogue!

ANTINOUS. I perhaps saw them without thinking about it, Lord. One of them left her veils floating up there on the terrace, for she was running . . .

THE EMPEROR. What are you doing, telling me that! Her veils! Her veils! What are that woman's veils to you! So why aren't you a woman yourself, knowing how to lie! Ah! She was running . . . why was she running?

ANTINOUS. To escape from the executioner, Lord! I can only tell you the truth, I am your slave.

THE EMPEROR. Quiet! You are a god! And you'll never be just a god, an idol, a monster, a creature born of the unknown. Your truths are lies since you keep inside you a heart full of silence. Nor do the gods speak . . . or they pronounce useless words which can be interpreted in a thousand ways. I don't want your respect, vile flute player! You've thrown me to fate. I'll find a way to punish you, even if I have to blind myself with my own sword. The soothsayers told me that a child would be born to the emperor Hadrian, a child who would slit his throat with a prostitute's nails. But I fear nothing. I'm not one of those Romans only interested in sensual delights, trembling with hunger and cold as soon as they leave Rome's bathhouses, I'm from wild Iberia, all my passions are acid and red as the blood of pomegranates! I shall make as many streams run red as I shall purify the waters of this cursed river . . . Oh Antinous! Antinous! I was hoping to cleanse myself in the peace of sleep and I shall no longer sleep since the eyes of women have fallen into the Nile! Have pity on your master! Console your king, my son! Think how I've given to those men who study the stars for my glory all the spoils of war, gold and silver; I've given them all the young male fruits gathered from the bosoms of the mothers prowling around my army's chariots. They sacrificed them in the crossroads of my gardens at the time of the waxing of the moon. And will I know what I want to know? Will the Jewish people be subjugated? Will I die in the hands of a courtesan? When I look at you, however, it is the charlatans that I want to see off. Are they not sicker than I am? They made me reduce to cinders—what an abomination—a ring of your hair in order to see into your thoughts. Antinous, will not their spirits be troubled by a deadly jealousy? You, a criminal? No! No! I would offend your divinity by suspecting you. Let us go that way. The banks are deserted. Yes, you're right, the wind is cooler. I would love to hear the reeds singing. What are those flowers floating like empty eggs? Where are your usual birds? The evening is peaceful. Ah! My beloved son, all calm comes from the shade. I hope from the darkness as I hope from you. Look! This is the mysterious moment. The stars are quivering, ready to flood your altar with their tears of joy. You are the god of joyful sadness and love's rain quenches the fevers. Yes, the sand is finer, paler, and its smooth slope plunges beneath the clear waves. Like a linen tunic drowned pleat by pleat. Oh! Those great lotus flowers raising their proud crowns. Greetings to you, my brothers, kings of the sacred river, chaste guardians of my treasure. Defend it!

Hold your stems in the shape of an arch, if you have touched its willowy spine, and cast your white corollas high so that they become azure as night falls! . . . They're drinking, the twin ibises, they're drinking, with their necks curved next to each other! Like two amphorae being filled one by one! They are drunk on life and that alone is all life's meaning! In vain, the science of my astrologers! The dizziness of battles has at last faded away in the reflection of your adorable body! Oh Antinous, don't go any further forward, don't disturb your reflexion! Let me contemplate the God's clear vision . . .

ANTINOUS. Don't lean over, Lord. The water is deep.

THE EMPEROR. I will kneel so I can lean over further, for all is permitted to the Emperor. No! The Egyptian Venus whose melancholically oval head is coveted by the golden hawk, the beautiful slim idol whose body seems to flee like a perfidious golden cord before prayers and offerings, the mother of all the Venuses because she remains a virgin, *Athara* herself, would be jealous of Antinous!

Listen my son, if I die I bequeath the empire to you. A god must be a king, that is to say the absolute master. The oracles have assured me that you dreamed of that. I wish it equally. You will find—I believe inside a square of flax which decorates my couch—a key, that of a very heavy small iron casket buried beneath the ninth column of your temple. This casket contains the *abaddir*, a stone as dark as the night, a stone fallen from the stars. When I'm dead, take it and reign! It is the strength of the prince who possesses it . . . Why are you turning your face away from me? Beyond the water did a woman excite you with her bleeding eyes? You were afraid! . . . The Jewesses! The Jewesses! Call my guards! My sword! Bring me my sword! So this evening I have drunk all the Nile's poisons! Call my soldiers so that they can whip this river with silken whips soaked in the moon's milk . . .

ANTINOUS. Oh, my Lord, you should go and rest!

THE EMPEROR. There is no more rest for your king. You have taken his power from him. There is no more freshness and the waves are sour: the heavens have filled them with salt. I no longer want to close my eyelids when the stars are opening upon you . . . Glory, what use are you to me? A child was born of my heart, he sprang from my breast, he rose up to my throat to smother me with his hands armed with pointed nails, with his prostitute's hands . . . and he looks at the Jewish girls watching him, cowering amongst the bank's lotus flowers. The executioner did not put out their eyes properly. Everything is badly done since Antinous came to reign . . . My son, find a sword so that I can kill those dead girls!

ANTINOUS. Excuse me Lord, but it's the time for bathing.

THE EMPEROR. Time for bathing? Ah! I see, I can be suffering from a fever, you, you go to bathe: you love the water's caresses much more than my words . . . you are so young! Go on . . . I'll wait . . . Your image! You blurred your image when you went into the river bed. Your beauty is disappearing, the god has left . . . Antinous! . . . Antinous! . . .

. . . Oh Nile, old Nile, father of metamorphoses, conqueror and master of the earth before me, I entreat you to keep the god's form or to give me back the goddess! By Athara, in the name of Love, change the sex of Antinous so that he can lie, so that he can be *a woman* when he comes back to me!

. . . And silence fell upon the dying roses.

THE BANQUET
OF THE GHOSTS
(*Socialism*)

For A-Ferdinand Herold[1]

TAKING the precautions of a man who knows the price of the slightest thing, this vagrant opened the small twist of paper containing his salt. He placed it on the checked handkerchief, his usual tablecloth which had already been used to wrap his bread, then he peeled an onion, a large onion, and started his meal. Lying on his stomach, with his legs disappearing beneath the grass, and his cap on the back of his neck, he dipped his onion in the salt, crunched it gently and swallowed huge crumbs of bread. As for the crust, he rubbed

---

1 French symbolist poet (1865-1940).

it very sanctimoniously, for he was convinced that he had to make the onion last as long as the bread.

It was a fine June day out in the countryside.

Right on the edge of the tablecloth, the spread-out handkerchief, was a forest of green brushwood, a forest full of busy insects, bellicose like armed men; tiny wild creatures, brown lice, red ant, flies with long probes, heaps of small voracious creatures with metallic bodices.

The first grain of salt which fell into the grass sparked a revolution; they busied about, quarrelled, and disappeared.

Superimposed upon the forest of brushwood, so huge when seen from close by, was another one beyond it, rising to the horizon, into the pure clarity of the sky, another one made of real trees which the distance of several leagues turned into toys. In the midst of these thick green woods a castle loomed, arising out of the wide lawns, an enormous castle the size of a military barracks judging by the absurd multiplicity of its windows, a colossal house fortified with terrace-gardens leading down to the river.

There was also a river, a wide river.

Between the forest of monstrous brushwood and that of miniature trees this distant watercourse offered a simple silver thread.

The calm atmosphere bathed all of that in a beauty which could give rise to tears.

The man finished his onion.

"It must be midday," he mused aloud.

His response was a bell chiming; not a solemn church bell, but a tinkling sound, imperious, shrill, manic, not counting its bongs, pealing back and forth at full tilt.

"What!" said the man, surprised.

The great silence was disturbed by this carillon, like a lake unsettled by the singing of its frogs.

"Ah! Ah!" thought the man. "They're going to have lunch at the chateau." And he added, shrugging his shoulders: "I expect they'll be tucking in up there!"

He wasn't a bad guy, but his frequent contacts with barracks and prisons had left him with a hatred of large buildings, particularly those which have no purpose.

As he was hungrily crunching his onion, enjoying his freedom, appreciative of his eternal wanderings which left him master of his actions and provided him with the amount of raw vegetables necessary for this robust stomach, he envisaged the feasting up there, calculated the number of courses, imagined the order of their sumptuous appearance (are there really no rich people who finish with soup!), their variety, the scarlet dishes, the tablecloths with their open-work embroidery, and the wine, above all the wine, flowing copiously like this river.

He angrily waved his hands and concluded:

"What a bunch of thieves, that rich lot!"

With his lunch finished, the checked handkerchief folded, the remaining salt placed carefully back in his pocket, he stood up, found his stick, twirled it around his head and murmured:

"What about going for a look."

He marched away.

Nothing better to do, anyway. Here and there, it didn't matter to him if he went in one direction or another.

He needed to find a bridge, and once he'd crossed the river he came up against the clever railings defending the woods and the park. At last he found a gap in a wall, climbed up, swearing, cursing, as if he was taking part in an assault.

In front of the main flight of steps leading up to the chateau, he was almost bowled over by its size. He was chilled to the marrow, that strange chill which you can't avoid in the presence of great lifeless objects.

Beneath his feet wide ruts led from the steps to the park gate, wide moss-covered ruts indicating that the last vehicles to have passed, strangely heavy and slow, were certainly heading a long way from the house.

The lawn, where flowers no longer grew, the wide, empty and dismal terraces, the great yawning windows opening their toothless mouths to the sun, the flights of steps grey with lichen, all suggested the negligence of footmen, a challenge tossed to the poor people:

they were so strong, those living here, that they were no longer afraid of being approached in a familiar way, of appearing rustic.

He climbed up, his stick in his hand, his cap over his eyes, scowling.

Sitting on one of the steps, a badly dressed old man was trimming a small potted rose bush. Around him more pots were placed at intervals; common wallflowers, a pale marigold, a thin white hyacinth, late flowering, with the look of a slim little girl wearing a loose dress.

The giant castle's thirty-six enormous mouths seemed now to be opening just to swallow these little pots.

The old fellow not having a mean look, the vagrant raised his cap:

"Without wishing to offend you, Monsieur," he said. "The weather is warm for this time of year. Could I ask you for a glass of wine?"

The old man smiled.

"Of plonk, yes my friend," he replied gently, very happy to talk to someone, "of plonk . . . no one has drunk wine here for a long time."

And they chatted whilst drinking two glasses of plonk on the marble staircase. It was finally *a sharing*.

"The owners are away?" asked the vagrant.

"The owners? There are none left!"

"And the chimes a little while ago, the lunch bell?" said the man, thinking he was being mocked and that the man was trying to get rid of him.

"No, my friend, there's only an old mad woman who obstinately refuses to sell and who is making a mistake as it is all falling into ruins. I am her servant because I'm much too old to move on. The work is not so hard, you see, with an eighty-year-old lady who can only manage milky gruel, and then by small spoonsful! Wine? It would make her ill just to smell it. As for me, I hardly take it. For that I'd need to be paid my back wages. Ah! The midday chimes? Mademoiselle is deaf, but she wants them to be sounded nevertheless: an old habit. She's very fussy about that. She likes to watch me pulling the rope; the rope moves more or less at her side up there, and she thinks she can hear it. She doesn't come downstairs, she doesn't go out, she lives under the eaves. No, of course, she doesn't eat lunch . . . In the dining room *there is never anyone!*"

The vagrant silently finished his glass of plonk, wiped his mouth with the back of his sleeve, went off murmuring rather a muffled thank you.

And all day he reflected on the *banquet of the ghosts* he had imagined in the great dining room of that dead castle.

A DOG'S LITTLE TEA PARTY
(*Anarchy*)

For Marcel Collière[1]

The white footpath curled beneath the dazzling sunlight around the lawn like the neck of an amorous swan. A bed of geraniums, trimmed with daisies like innumerable silver stars, placed upon the velvety green of the lawn a huge ruby, and the great setting of the ring which seemed to contain it showed a pearly setting of delicate gems. Gently, to either side of the mowed grass, stylish trees, those old heralds of arms, grouped to allow a view, in the background, of the clear façade of a mansion resembling an opera house, a

---

1 French poet (1863-1932).

milky building whose windows, each with a single pane, released a glow like diamonds. Flights of steps, decorated with an openwork design, the slender scrolls here and there of an overly modern ironwork, gilded like a gold-smith's workshop, stretched their jewel-laden arms towards the potential visitor. Coming down from there in gentle cascades, carpets of violent hues poured multi-coloured tidal waves into the pale streams of the pathways, whose studied lines stretched out until they disappeared towards the park's gate, a gigantic festive gate, a monument crowned with bronze urns where flowering cacti thrust up into the sky their fierce purple iron spears.

The sky, of a smooth totally pure azure, warmed and caressed all these objects with an unstoppable determination.

There was no-one.

There was no trace of footsteps along the pathways.

The flowers had no fragrance, flowers of painted metal which had been placed there to make waiting easier.

Waiting for fairies? Or for kings?

At one of the curtainless windows could be seen the natural silhouette of a footman, but which seemed illusory because of the parting of his black hair, straight as a die like the pale footpaths of the park, the range of copper buttons decorating his waistcoat, the impassive respectfulness of his movements, gently shaking an enormous ostrich feather like the plume of a hearse.

Yet just a little beyond the copse to the left, in a clump of tamarisks where a rustic table had been set up beneath a canvas sunshade, two human beings were playing, trying to lead a life despite the setting.

Two children.

A little girl of eight.

A little boy a year older.

They were, like their opera house of a home, extraordinarily pretty.

These two children, overwhelmed by the heat and the wealth heaped upon them by heaven, were looking at pictures, peacefully.

"When we've finished the book, we'll start it again," said the little boy, gently bossy.

"Yes, but we'll start it again *from the middle*," added the little girl, already becoming capricious.

A luxurious album, this book in which the queens and the female saints had robes of powdered gold, the soldiers arms were embossed and even the beggars were wearing new rags, especially made.

It was admirable.

The captions, inscribed below the pictures, came from long ago.

This one for instance, spreading beneath the portrait of a lady giving something to drink to poor people: *"You should always do good, because you will always be rewarded."*

The children were not reading, too busy with the shimmering colours of the characters.

Sometimes they yawned.

The little girl was wearing a dress of embroidered muslin, very simple, a blouse with wide soft pleats, but the embroidery, entirely hand stitched, must have cost the eyesight of several seamstresses.

The little boy, wearing a manly sailor's uniform, showed his bare neck, a little tanned because of the season and running around without a hat, and a vest of Indian silk which had come by sea from countries where you buy them along with yellow fever, if not with cholera.

The two children were hardly laughing.

They were thinking, leafing through the book, their gaze misted by futile dreams.

Lying around behind them, abandoned long ago, were the props of a comedy long since finished, a huge doll, almost the sister of the little girl, fairly modestly dressed, a baby with an enamel head with pupils of sapphires and medals won at an exhibition, and a game of skittles whose satin balls did no harm and made no sound.

The little girl was blonde, pretty, with scars close to her neck. Her eyes, brighter and bigger than those of the doll, resembled two goblets of pure water.

The little boy, dark-haired, chubbier, still had the sad mouth of those who have had too much cod liver oil to drink.

They were both a little bored with having to amuse themselves every day.

Suddenly, as they were about to open the book *at the middle*, they could hear shouting.

The great silence which engulfed the opera house and its setting was suddenly no more, because something was finally happening.

From the distance, by the garden gate, a tumult of voices, of people going by, a troop of people hurrying along, very angry people . . .

A sort of dull growling . . . then nothing.

The gate, pushed by an unseen arm, seemed to shake, to move aside blocking the view, and then closed again.

"What's that coming in?" said the little girl.

"Nobody," replied the little boy, sadly. "It was beggars trying to get in. They weren't able to."

He well knew that you couldn't get in there like that.

"But something has," cried the little girl (and the goblets of pure water of her eyes lit up with enthusiasm), "something came in! Look! It's a big animal, is it a wolf?"

She well knew that there are no wolves; however, she always hoped to meet one.

It was a dog.

The two children came out of the clump of trees, sniffing excitement.

The dog went along the main pathway, the very one that circled the lawn like a swan's amorous neck. He trotted along sideways, his ears and tail hanging low, his tongue lolling. He limped with one of his hind legs, and his rust-coloured coat was not clean.

He stopped, arriving at the geranium bed; leaving the path's sinuous track, he made straight for the lawn, stopped again in front of shining and well-raked sand of the other path, stumbled again, and joined the children who were amazed by his behaviour.

"Poor dog, he's been beaten," said the little girl.

"I think he's bleeding," added the little boy.

On his side an open wound was dribbling black drops, more of mud than of blood.

"Poor doggy!" said the little girl, her heart tightening.

"Poor doggy!" said the little boy, also moved because his sister was laying on the sleeve of his sailor suit her little hand trembling with compassion.

The dog hesitated, lowering his head further, seeming to consider.

A tough job, his.

In his vacant, almost gentle, eyes, to which fever had given a faraway look, was all the despair of what he was going to do, of what he was *forced* to do.

It wasn't his fault. No. In the grip of a mysterious illness, a supernatural power, he had been running for weeks, carrying out a shady mission, and ashamed, cringing, his tongue hanging out, he scrutinised the children.

In ordinary times he would have liked to play with them.

He didn't hate children. He even preferred them to men.

He had been prodded with forks, pushed up by chance to this gate and the kind God of animals, by letting him enter this paradise, perhaps wanted to set him on another path. He made himself seem modest, small.

And yet he felt that neither the beauty of the site or of the children, nor the sanctity of the haven being offered to him, would stop him . . .

"He must be thirsty," sighed the little girl, fascinated by the poor dog.

"Wait! I'll fetch him something to drink," declared the little boy; and he ran off towards the mansion.

When he came back, accompanied by the tall footman, carrying a bowl of milk on a silver platter, the little girl, standing in the same place, was all alone.

Her eyes, brimming with tears, looked more and more like two goblets of pure water, ready to overflow.

"Where is the dog?" cried the little boy.

The little one replied, trembling a little:

"He ran away, he didn't want to wait . . . because I scolded him. He's a naughty dog."

She hiccupped.

"What's wrong, Mademoiselle?" asked the tall footman, anxiously.

The little girl cuddled up to her brother, turning away.

"You mustn't say anything," she murmured, "or they'll beat him again! He bit me, here on the thumb, not very much . . . the mark has already gone away. He has very little strength, you see? . . . It didn't hurt me but it upset me, that's all."

That must have upset the naughty dog too. But the supernatural fever which tortures these dogs leaves no room for pity.

They are on a mission.

"We won't say anything," replied the little boy with innocent conceit.

And he blew upon his sister's thumb.

THE LAST TEMPTATION

For Pierre Quillard[1]

AND from the north came a gust of wind, whistling round the presbytery, furiously buffeting the four corners of its grey walls.

"When the wind blows," murmured the oldest of the three priests with a sigh, "I imagine small boats on the open sea. I see them turning, dancing; I say to myself: 'they're gone, but they're in the hands of the Saviour!' Labussière, will you take some more of these quenelles? We must please Augustine, because

---

1 Pierre Quillard (1864-1912) was a French symbolist poet, playwright and journalist.

the good woman has been bustling around her stoves for you since this morning. We don't do this every day. I myself don't eat, or very little."

Father Labussière held out his plate. The old Amblars priest added: 'That was a great show, this morning's first communions.'

Across his amiable face passed something like a light zigzag of lightning.

"Yes," said Father Jorit, "but the passion is fading. The parents attend without taking part in the moving ceremony, which is less moving. The grown-ups are losing interest."

"Our provinces are being poisoned by socialism."

"Reverend Father, in Paris where socialism reigns, all the churches are full on Sundays."

"I can believe that," he said mischievously, "they enjoy shows in Paris!"

He wiped his mouth.

That was the end of their discussion about their calling.

The Amblars priest looked up at the ceiling, seeking something. Augustine had forgotten to remove the gauze cover from the chandelier. It was not a pretty sight, those copper branches imprisoned beneath a piece of dirty yellowish material, looking like the metallic canvas of a meat safe. However, the room was taking shape, thanks to reflections from the fire blazing in the large hearth. It was well polished, very clean; the grey flowers against a grey background of the wallpaper had the look of clouds against a dying sunset. A Christ and a Virgin Mary were disappearing against the distant crowned heads of birds of prey. Thick bronze damask curtains covered the windows, decorated with a garland, a tapestry by the young ladies of the convent of Saint Theresa. Two large oil lamps sent up two vertical flames. It felt warm.

On the table were spread all the riches of the old cupboards: damask linen scented with citronella, heavy silverware, ornamental cutlery which filled your hands as you ate, dishes of matching white porcelain, the clear clay a little chipped around the edges but showing a solid antiquity. The bottles, slightly dusty, placed on china saucers that had lost their cups, were in a sombre row: Médoc, Sauternes and the last of the Rhine wine lavishly wrapped and placed in a very delicate little basket. The glasses had a special blue tint, disguising the shades of the wines by their bases frosted with azure droplets. The sauces gave off a delicious aroma. They were eating meat quenelles arranged like a flock of shapeless chickens around a crusty hen, the hen so golden that it looked like a sham. To the left of the main course and to its right were, in no particular order, boxed cold small birds, their feet hanging over the curled edge of the paper giving a touching impression of gentle martyrs, and cucumbers stuffed with breadcrumbs soaked in milk. A blancmange waited on the dresser behind them, its creaminess surrounded by an army of very dry petit fours.

The Amblars priest only nibbled. Around his plate was a black crowd of ants: the tobacco he was consuming.

This evening he was very worried about his dog, a *Finnoise*,[1] about to give birth. The doctor and the lawyer were keeping one each.

---

1 Finnish Lapphund, a hardy, easy going, medium-sized breed, traditionally used for herding reindeer in its native country, Finland.

They would be obliged to get rid of the others. He loved animals.

Father Labussière was drinking happily, quickly, without worrying about the wine or the age on the bottles.

Father Jorit, younger, was studying the dates whilst warming the frosted base of his glass, calculating, sniffing, then forgetting to drink whilst he ate.

Madame Augustine appeared, bringing a Russian salad in an ordinary salad bowl (the white salad bowl had been broken). Nasturtium flowers depicted an orange velvet arabesque upon portions of vegetables divided into beams of starlight. She put down the dish respectfully. She was a thin woman, wearing Carmelite wool, a black silk apron, a fluted bonnet. She retained an appearance of freshness, conscious of her links to the church, took care of herself and every Sunday morning, after scouring the saucepans, before the first masses, she would remove her earrings, two golden pears, and brush them in soapy water with a nailbrush.

The three priests recognised her skill and respected it. Her despair was to be serving an old man who was incapable of distinguishing a fattened chicken from a capon.

They complimented her in familiar terms.

"Another dish! But that's a devilish temptation!" exclaimed Jorit.

"Quenelles, Madame Augustine, wonderful quenelles!" said Labussière.

And the old Amblars priest, nodding his head in agreement, realised, not without some surprise, that they had asked for more.

"It's like being with Monseigneur," concluded Jorit.

Madame Augustine lowered her eyes, her cheekbones reddening with pride; but her only response was to serve the salad.

There was a moment of bliss.

. . . And the north wind sent down a more furious gust which closed the shutters with a bang, shaking the whole house.

"Speaking of which: my dog?" said the old priest, worried. "Has she got straw? Has she got soup? Are you seeing to her, Madame

Augustine? That wind must be bothering her! How is she doing?"

"She's well, Reverend Father. The time is near. She's sniffing the straw, turning it over! Oh! A real little family home in her kennel!"

"The *Finnoise*," said Jorit, "is a beautiful animal. The coat is so white! Does she catch partridges?"

"A pointer if you like," said Labussière, "an amateur, but made evil by the wind, gets carried away hither and thither, like a Russian dog. It will get you regardless a rabbit or a wolf! Its nose is too hot, it even chases butterflies. Too much oomph."

"Allow me! Allow me!" fussed the old priest, anxiously. "My *Finnoise* looks after me."

"Ah!" exclaimed Labussière, getting worked up, "the dogs of Doctor Carjol, our député, what a nasty pack! Yesterday, the hunt passed close to my presbytery with its hunting horns. Thirty beaters, and they unearthed nothing much. All that noise . . ."

The old priest sat up.

"Your député! You know, he's not mine. He plays the great lord, and he wears a red coat like a monkey's. A bad situation, his scandal in Issoire.[1]"

Suavely, Jorit tasted the Sauternes.

"Reverend Father," he said gaily, "people are so vilified in the departmental press that you don't know where you stand. Is it the factory, is he right? For me, I think they haven't studied the map: the agreement should have been done away with first, then the priory, and as for the domestic waste, in principal it should always be channelled away. On paper, there is always the right to purification."

And he laughed.

"I don't agree with you," the old priest, shaken, risked saying with little doddery gestures; "that poor Voreuse priest is like me: changing his habits at his age, it's murder! Come on, come on, his life won't be long! Yes! The young député should be ashamed. They're all young now . . . too young!"

And a physical hatred showed in his kind eyes for those who live life to the full.

Labussière shrugged his shoulders.

---

1 A commune in the Auvergne.

"For me," he said, "I would have demolished it, but I would have rebuilt straightaway. As for the convent school, it wasn't directly linked, there was a squalid little street separating it from the secondary school where the pupils came throwing so much filthy rubbish . . ."

They argued for a moment like very well brought up hugely obstinate people. Jorit quoted some text of a speech by a local councillor. Labussière punctuated it with a light blow of his fist on the tablecloth, whilst gripping his fork seriously. They all drank at the same time.

The dessert was brought, and Augustine went out to go and see the dog, because the Amblars priest was grieving.

She came straight back, frightened.

"Reverend Father," she said hoarsely, "there's someone asking for you."

"My God, who?"

And the old man flinched. He'd arrived at the point where enemies are seen everywhere. The two others, intrigued, perked up.

"It's a priest . . . that I don't know. And . . . look . . . he's here . . . he's here!"

She took refuge behind the table as the wind, sweeping in through the door from the garden, roughly flattened the lamps' flames, shattering one of the glasses. Acrid smoke vomited from the chimney spread around, blue-coloured, punchy, and a chill suddenly increased the heat as the spirit of icy water increases the spirit of hot water in a boiler. At the door appeared something like a pale curtain: the overcoat of the new priest, a strange coat, with rigid pleats, made of a greyish yellow material, almost white, the dress-coat of a missionary or an almoner from a far-away place. This priest looked tall because he held his head high. He certainly wore a cassock, but had no tonsure. His body, hardly supple, not moving, looked like a tree trunk, like a formidable and mysterious being, sheathed in wood. He greeted them and moved forward, revealing a slightly scarred forehead, lacerated by one of those interesting wounds from blows either of a sabre or of the claws which only tigers have. His eyes were those of a pure child, of a happy and chaste woman, sparkling, with bushy eyelashes beneath whose shade the blue corollas of his pupils blossomed like two flowers emerging from the darkness of a well. His nose, shaped like the prow of an ancient Norman boat, deeply lined along the nostrils, as if placed on the face by two sharp chisel points, gave him an aggressive look; yet he had a kind mouth, tender, a little full, which he had to keep biting with his large teeth, with all the ferocity of those with ambition.

"I am," he said with a firm voice, "the priest of Voreuse. I thank you, gentlemen, for your kind welcome. The wind is terrible this evening. I am on my way on foot from the main station to my new parish, and the roads are really bad. What a country! Would you allow me to rest for an hour?"

Labussière and Jorit, inwardly charmed to be able to fulfil their holy obligations towards the guest, straightaway took one his hat, the other his white coat. Augustine, entranced, refreshed the flames, threw on some logs, but the Amblars priest, the old man, exclaimed in horror.

"I don't know you! You're not the Voreuse priest, you're young!"

They looked at each other: Augustine seized a plate from the table with the remains of the blancmange and quickly removed it.

The Voreuse priest smiled.

"Ah!" he said lightly, "of course . . . the other one, the first *me*, is dead!"

Exclamations flew around. They were all speaking at once, very enlivened by the generous wines and by a grief which resembled pleasure, as our neighbour's death is nothing other than a danger that we have not experienced. They were scornful of the Issoire député, discussing the placing on the map of the priory and offering drinks. The new priest studied them: he refused the glass of Sauternes and accepted a cup of coffee without sugar.

"Really," he said, a little sardonically, "did you not suspect his end? He died yesterday, at dawn, because his praying-desk, his prie-Dieu had been moved. He could not pray to the north-east."

There was a general stupor. The Amblars priest wept, very moved. Finally, that word, *Dieu,* restored order. They made the sign of the cross, like those remembering in the depths of their misery that somewhere there is a very decent rich man who will lend them what they need to meet their immediate needs. Then the smoke dissipated a little, and they questioned the traveller. He had come from far in fact; he even confessed that intellectually, he came from Rome, speaking in a strangely calm, singing tone, daring with certain turns of phrase to utter the pleasantries of a man of the world; but beneath the cloak of his words he remained enigmatic.

"We're being murdered! Save us, Lord!" exclaimed the Amblars priest, alluding to the death of the old Voreuse priest.

"Believe me, gentlemen," responded the new arrival, "we commit suicide far more than we are murdered. There are other means of preserving the respect we are owed, I swear to you."

"Religious fervour is fading away!"

"There are flames which are never extinguished . . . And if, by any chance, I had discovered a system, if I proposed that you should use it, would you accept, would you try it? Tell me, gentlemen, for I see you are ready for anything, as your sacred fervour has heated up as you have heated up this poor chilled traveller?"

"It's of no use, deep in our countryside, Reverend priest of Voreuse" continued Jorit with a discreet laugh.

The stranger stood up and gazed around him with his flowery look.

"Nothing is of no use, Monsieur. It was especially deep in the wild forests that long ago the bloody rites took place, the fearful sacrifices to redeem our races. You don't think that Saint Bernard's Rules, in their minute details, renewed with another Rule, is something futile? And, speaking theologically, it was a small rectification which had an enormous influence wasn't it! Listen carefully to me, the time and the complicated mysteries of this night mean that we are coming closer to each other, that we're becoming brothers, *accomplices for goodness*. Who knows whether we'll ever see each other again. I am telling you this in the confidence of the confessional: the Voreuse priest committed suicide! . . . Oh, don't wave your arms around so madly! I know it! I'm the only one who knows. I guessed it, he fell coming home, on a new step which his feet had not yet got used to, I think he meant to fall, he gave way, do you understand? I, a missionary soul . . . a preacher in the desert, sometimes I am charged with purifying the desecrated place by slowly expatiating on the future works, whose beginnings are an imperceptible change of direction. I seek out simple souls and faithful hearts to work with me on this transformation of matter, *the matter of the Holy Spirit!*"

He was standing straight, without moving, amongst them like a tree struck by lightning, completely black, upon which two late flowers still blossomed, the double flower of his voluptuous gaze. He was no longer laughing, for he was officiating.

"Listen, my brothers, for too long out of a habit unblessed by any divine order, for a misunderstood and lethal idea of universality, matter has stuck to a direction it should not have. From small beginnings great ideas grow, you know that! Since, in the end, form has to represent substance, since the contract cannot be obliterated nor the writings changed, the only thing one can do is to bring love's sharp blade into this thousand-year-old parchment! We must try this small act of madness which will perhaps become the great wisdom of future nations!" (And at this point the speaker drew himself up as if enlightened.) "*Gentlemen, the Host should be OVAL!* . . . and do you know why it's round? No-one knows! Consult the texts and leaf through all the books reputed to be sacred! You won't find out. The first one was a piece of bread, very ordinary. The shape of a piece of bread is not laid down. The Host was made round *automatically*. Reasonably, logically, it should be *oval*. I repeat, in truth, there is nothing against that, and on the contrary, everything ordains it. I believe that in order to entice the small mouths of women and children the body of Christ needs to lengthen a little, like the cross, to the shape of an egg! It was made round, the Host, like the earth, but they forgot that the earth, with its unknown poles, flattens and hides in the line of its circumference as if in a mysterious refuge of evolution. The Host should be oval! You are too busy with the small points of your calling to forget that one. Gentlemen, my brothers,

I have the Pope's permission, my system is guaranteed, and before the eyes of ordinary people, without too many explanations, we shall introduce the oval Host. There will be the attraction of the new, of unease! They will want to see the body of Christ, of the Saviour who has changed! As for us, we'll see the women and children kneel more submissively! The Host must be oval . . ."

Overwhelmed, the old Amblars priest nodded, his gaze distant. The two other priests, demoralised, were lost in uncomprehending thought.

"You have the papal brief?" asked Jorit, slightly nonplussed by the lack of documentation.

"It's a major development!" concluded Labussière enthusiastically.

The stranger smiled.

"Gentlemen, I'm leaving you. With our common outlook, tomorrow, at your low mass, think of me!"

He picked up his white overcoat, his dark hat and quickly left.

The weather had calmed down, it was raining heavily, but Augustine came back, very upset. "Reverend Father," she said, trembling all over, "you are going to be very sad! The *Finnoise* has just given birth; but someone, frightening her, has made her ferocious, she's eaten her little ones."

And the three priests, for the second time, crossed themselves.

PRIMORDIAL NAKEDNESS

AND now amongst the luxuriant leafiness of the paradise on earth appears the last fruit to have ripened beneath the hand of God.

And now from burning furnace of the man's breast has appeared this loaf of white flesh, these soft crumbs, wrapped in the auburn corn of her straw hair, a promise of all the future harvests to undulate beneath the sun's rays!

O fruit-flower! Peach of the profane! Rose of dawn! Blood of strawberries or black grapes! Wine of triumphal killings and libation of sacrifices!

O bread of voluptuousness, supreme good, sacred food of the poor, cake of kings, you who satiate or unleash the appetite!

O woman, you who carry all joys in the hollow of your two hands and support with the two columns of your legs of marble the mysterious crucible of human destinies!

God is resting.

The man is sleeping.

Satan is watching and awaiting, behind the tree of knowledge, the opportunity to disturb the serenity of this moment.

Eve, our mother, our mistress and our friend, Eve, our salvation, our perdition and our redemption, open your heavenly eyes upon the infancy of the world.

Completely naked, with no covering other than her hair which she tosses behind her in order to better contemplate the divine spectacle of this first morning of this first springtime, she watches, dazzled and even more dazzling in her amazement at receiving the accolades of creation. For all creatures have come in humility to prostrate themselves and to lick her feet: the lion, the tiger, the bear, the monkey, the dog, both the greatest and the smallest . . .

She stretches out her open hands to their multiple caresses, admires them. What beautiful furs, what soft tongues of red flame and how she will love them because they'll be faithful allies!

. . . But what a shame it is that amongst all these animals with their innocent power, their unconscious strength, there is not one capable of standing up straight on two legs, upright to the height of her lips so that she can return its kiss . . . which she invents!

Satan, the serpent, wrapped around the colossal trunk of this tree whose roots reach down to hell and whose palms spread up to the highest heavens, tightens his rings which make a strange grinding sound. The piecing gaze upon Eve of the emerald eyes in his triangular head is like a weapon, a silent threat.

And on high, the worried birds are flapping their wings, singing, whistling their short melancholic warnings.

The nightingale sings happily, and the dove weep.

Eve smiles at the serpent, as she smiled at the others.

Why doesn't he prostrate himself? He's made for crawling after all.

He has beautiful eyes and the curves of his supple body, with no limbs to move him along, are a wonderful shape, harmonising with his round hips, on his own he is as beautiful as several necklaces!

From the tree's branches creepers, festoons droop: garlands of orchids, branches of wild vines.

Satan dangles beneath these arcs of greenery, seems to be seeking something to lean on even though his rings clinging to the tree are as solid as metal.

Is he really going to be the only one who doesn't bow before her radiant majesty, continuing his strange dance around her, trying to control her with his triangular head?

Eve is amazed and offended by this lack of respect. Adam is still sleeping. God, giving way to the fatigue of his seventh day of labour, is perhaps forgetting . . .

He doesn't even have time to foresee his enemy's ploy.

The serpent has found what he was seeking! His head, a monstrous dagger, a wide steel blade glinting with blues and greens, has just cut with its poisonous fangs into a leaf of the wild vine whose loops are hanging above him. His emerald eyes, suddenly closed, hide a dreadful thought: he offers, not as was thought long ago, an apple, a fruit, to Eve who has taken a curious interest in his dubious manoeuvres, but *a leaf*, a triangular imitation of his own face, *a vine leaf* which he finally poses gently, with his eyes still closed, upon the small blonde triangle which seals with a seal of pure gold the smooth white belly of the first woman . . .

She herself stops smiling, then lowers her eyelids, intimidated.

Because our mother, Eve, has closed her eyes in full daylight, the sky has darkened . . . The birds, frightened, fall silent. All the animals lying on the grass leap up and flee in a frenzy. In the distance the ocean roars with anger. It is the revolt of the elements, the end of Eden, the storm . . .

Fear has made its entrance into the world which is being shaken by dreadful shivering. God and thunder start to growl! At this infernal noise the man awakens, not understanding what is happening. He rises, finally noticing this beautiful mysterious creature standing before him, hiding her face behind her hair.

. . . Modesty is born with the first gesture of shame, and humanity is condemned to the eternal misery of clothing . . .

Oh sacred nakedness! Primordial nakedness!

www.ingramcontent.com/pod-product-compliance
Lightning Source LLC
Chambersburg PA
CBHW020231120726
47903CB00008B/2635